Ellen Ochoa

Ellen Ochoa grew up in California. Today she has an exciting job. She is an astronaut.

First day of sixth grade

Ellen posing with some birthday gifts

Ellen receiving a Ph.D. degree

She works for the National Aeronautics and Space Administration, or NASA.

Ellen training at the Johnson Space Center for her space flights

Ellen with astronaut Joseph P. Tanner

Ellen Ochoa has gone on two space flights.

On her first space flight, Ellen was part of the crew of *Discovery:* (seated) Stephen S. Oswald, Kenneth D. Cameron; (standing) Kenneth D. Cockrell, Michael Foale, Ellen Ochoa.

On her second space flight, Ellen wore a patch like this on her space suit.

She studied the sun. She used the shuttle's robot arm to pick up a satellite.

Ochoa aboard *Discovery*

One of Ellen's hobbies is flying a small airplane.

Another hobby is playing the flute. She is shown here at a 1989 recital and taking a break in space.

Ellen likes to speak to children. She tells them to work hard. If they do, they can be what they want to be.

Ellen Ochoa is a good example to others. She worked hard to reach her goals.

Ellen Ochoa likes being an astronaut. "There's nothing else I'd rather be doing," she says.

Let's Explore!

Ellen Ochoa and other astronauts work and study at the Johnson Space Center in Texas. Find the Johnson Space Center on the map. Follow Ellen's route from the Space Center to where the liftoff happened.

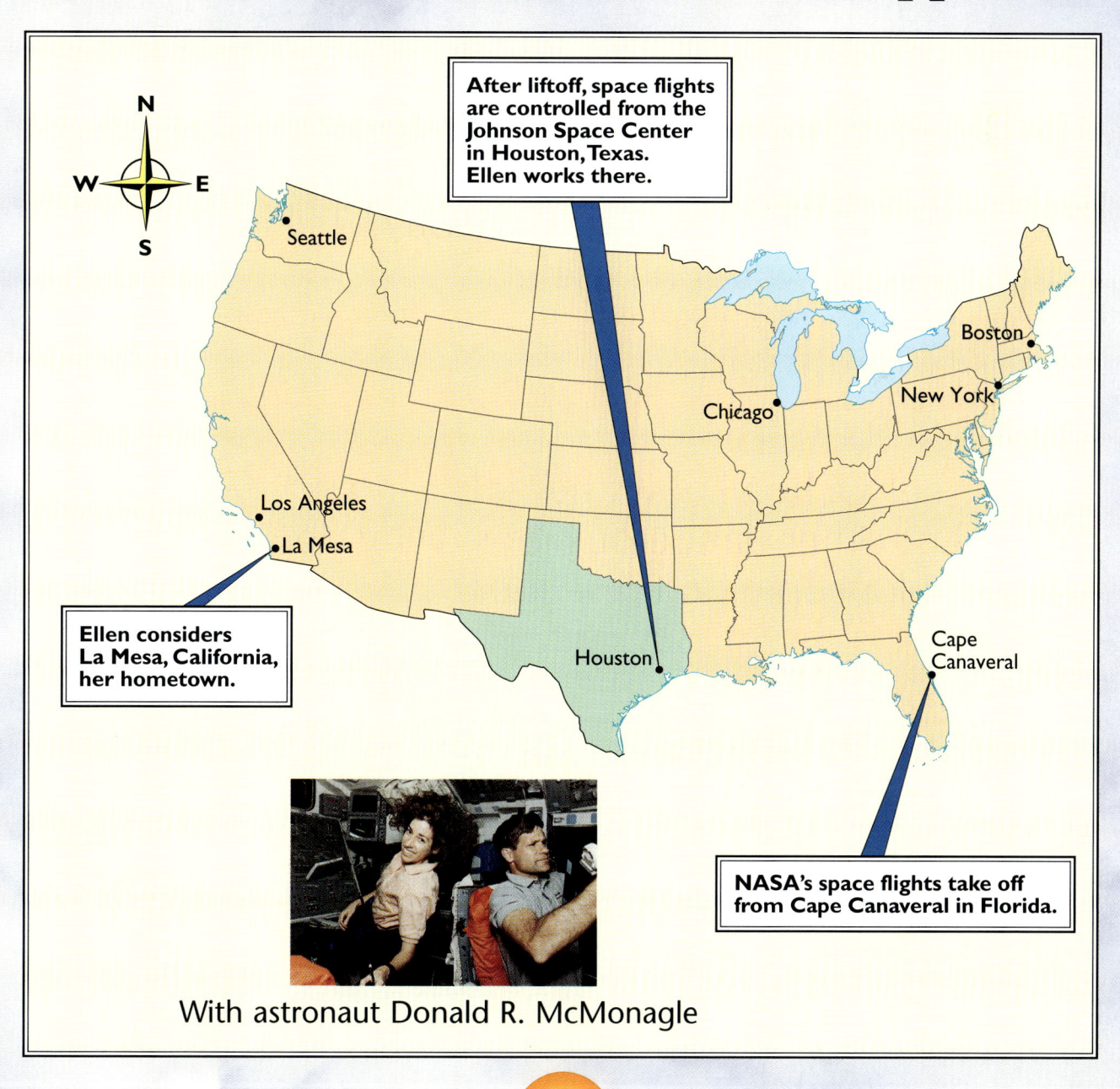

After liftoff, space flights are controlled from the Johnson Space Center in Houston, Texas. Ellen works there.

Seattle

Chicago

Boston

New York

Los Angeles

La Mesa

Houston

Cape Canaveral

Ellen considers La Mesa, California, her hometown.

NASA's space flights take off from Cape Canaveral in Florida.

With astronaut Donald R. McMonagle

9

What Do You Think?

In Space
Imagine that you have been invited to go along on a space flight. Would you like to go to the moon? To a star? Somewhere else? Write a picture story about it.

Attention, All Inventors!
Besides being an astronaut, Ellen Ochoa is a scientist and an inventor. What do you hope someone will invent someday? Tell a friend why it would be useful.

Danger Ahead!
Astronaut Ochoa knows her job can be risky. List other dangerous jobs. Why do you think people do these jobs?

I Can Make a Difference!
Ellen likes to speak to children in schools. She said, "That's where I can make a difference." Tell about something else people can do to make a difference.

Take a Look!

From the space shuttle, Ellen Ochoa could see exciting views of Earth.

Recording an ocean scene aboard *Discovery*

Mexico and the United States

Africa, Asia, Europe

Hawaiian Islands

Storm clouds

Key Events

Ellen and her family

1958 Ellen Ochoa was born in Los Angeles, California.

1975 She graduated from high school in La Mesa, California.

1980 She was top student of San Diego State University in California.

1985 She graduated from Stanford University in Palo Alto, California.

1991 She became an astronaut for NASA.

1993 From April 8 to 17, she was on her first space flight.

1994 From November 3 to 14, she was on her second space flight.

The *Discovery* crew